This Walker book belongs to:

_____

_____

First published 1989 by Walker Books Ltd, 87 Vauxhall Walk, London SE11 5HJ

This edition published 2021

2 4 6 8 10 9 7 5 3 1

This book has been typeset in Bembo

Printed in China

British Library Cataloguing in Publication Data:
a catalogue record for this book is available from the British Library

ISBN 978-1-4063-9591-4

www.walker.co.uk

Old Mother Hubbard's Dog
Learns to Play

John Yeoman
Quentin Blake

WALKER BOOKS
AND SUBSIDIARIES
LONDON · BOSTON · SYDNEY · AUCKLAND

Said Old Mother Hubbard, while swatting some flies,

"You shouldn't sit reading all day.

They say that it's terribly bad for the eyes.

I do wish you'd learn how to play."

While Old Mother Hubbard was reading her post
And sorting out letters and bills,
She heard – and the sound made her white as a ghost –
The dog, with a flute, playing trills.

The dog took a cello to play in the hall;
The music was squawky and shrill.
It twisted the hands of the clock on the wall
And made the canary quite ill.

So Old Mother Hubbard went out for a bone
And peeped in around the back door;
She saw that the dog had got out a trombone
And was blowing the rugs off the floor.

Said Old Mother Hubbard, "I really don't know
What to do with a dog with such faults."
The dog, in the kitchen, with fiddle and bow,
Was teaching the mice how to waltz.

Said Old Mother Hubbard, "That terrible din
Is making my rose bushes wilt."
The dog, with his bagpipes, strolled by with a grin
And gave her a wave with his kilt.

Then Old Mother Hubbard climbed up in a tree:
"Perhaps I should pick him some plums.
If I give him a few – with a nice cup of tea –
I might stop him playing those drums."

What else he was planning, she hadn't a clue:
She felt much too nervous to look.
While the dog settled down, for an hour or two,
And quietly got on with his book.

The Adventures of Old Mother Hubbard's Dog

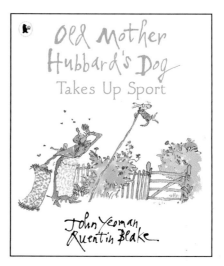

Also illustrated by Quentin Blake

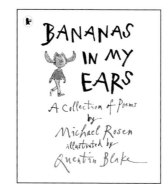

Available from all good booksellers

www.walker.co.uk